This Little Hippo
book belongs to

_____

_____

To Francesco
V.P.

Scholastic Children's Books,
Commonwealth House, 1-19 New Oxford Street,
London WC1A 1NU, UK
a division of Scholastic Ltd

London • New York • Toronto • Sydney • Auckland

First published by Little Hippo,
an imprint of Scholastic Ltd, 1999

Text copyright © Joan Stimson, 1999
Illustrations copyright © Valeria Petrone, 1999

ISBN 0 590 11413 1

Printed in Italy by Amadeus S.p.A. - Rome

Basil
and the
Babysitters

by Joan Stimson
illustrated by Valeria Petrone

Little Hippo

Basil was a crocodile. A smiley, well-behaved crocodile.
But Basil couldn't keep a babysitter.

When his parents went to the Swamp Slither,
Uncle Chomp was in charge.

"Try my home-made toffee," said Basil politely.

But the toffee was stickier than it looked. Uncle Chomp was still chewing when Basil's parents came back.

"This toffee is disgusting!" said Uncle Chomp.
"I think he means – DON'T ASK ME AGAIN!" sighed Basil's mum.

Another night Basil's parents had a dinner date.
And Cousin Tina came round.

But, as soon as Basil went to bed, Tina could hear strange noises.

"WHOOOH! WHOOOH!"

Basil was playing dinosaurs – extra quietly – just like his parents had told him.

Poor Tina thought it was a ghost.
"DON'T ASK ME AGAIN!" wailed Tina when Basil's
parents came back.

Basil was sorry to lose another babysitter.

For a while Mum and Dad found it easier to stay in.

But then they heard about the Keep Fit Classes.
"We mustn't miss those!" they agreed.
And this time they asked Big Boris to babysit.

"Here's my son," smiled Basil's mum.
"And here's my pet spider," smiled Basil.
WHOOOOSH! Big Boris didn't like spiders.

"DON'T ASK ME AGAIN!" he yelled over his shoulder.

That night Mum went to Keep Fit on her own.

Dad stayed at home and looked disappointed.

Basil was disappointed too.

"Shall we have our favourite story?" he asked Dad.

Next week it was Dad's turn to go out while
Mum looked after Basil. Afterwards Dad rushed
home with exciting news.
"I've met someone at Keep Fit," cried Dad.
"And his daughter loves babysitting.
But no one ever asks her."

Basil's parents couldn't wait to go to Keep Fit together. And Basil was keen to meet his new babysitter.

So on the day of the next class no one wanted anything to go wrong. "This toffee is disgusting!" said Mum at breakfast. But she still made them eat it all up.

"AAAARGH!" roared Dad. "Let's be dinosaurs all day.
Then Basil can be himself this evening."

And just before the new babysitter was due,
Basil hid his spider.

Mum, Dad and Basil all waited eagerly for the new babysitter to arrive. Suddenly, Basil had a dreadful thought.

"What if she's extra nervous?" he cried.

"And that's why no one ever asks her?"

"SHUSH!" said Basil's parents.

"She'll hear you."

And at that moment the new babysitter
bounced in the door.
"Hello," she boomed in a friendly voice. "I'm Beverley.
And these," she went on, "are my pet spiders!"

By the time Mum and Dad left for Keep Fit,
Basil was being a brontosaurus.
"NEEOOW!" Beverley was being a pterodactyl.

And when Mum and Dad came back, they found that the 'dinosaurs' had been busy in the kitchen.

"This toffee is lovely!" slurped Beverley.
Basil bounced round and round his parents.
He had something exciting to tell them.

"I think she means – ASK ME AGAIN!"
said Basil.